W9-BNE-346

16.95

SHOWDOWN ON THE SMUGGLER'S MOON: VOLUME 5

It is a period of renewed hope for the Rebellion. Luke Skywalker's quest to learn the ways of the Jedi brought him to the infamous moon Nar Shaddaa, where his lightsaber made him a quick target for the Jedi artifact collector GRAKKUS THE HUTT, and he is now being held prisoner.

After Sana Solo – the woman who claims to be Han's wife – rescued the smuggler and Princess Leia from Imperial fire, Leia received a distress call from the rebel fleet informing them of Luke's predicament. Meanwhile, C-3PO and Chewbacca have already arrived on the Smuggler's Moon in search of their friend.

However, with a new bounty hunter on the tail of the Wookiee warrior, the rebels must get to Luke before Grakkus and the Gamemaster send him to the arena and a fight to the death....

JASON AARON
Writer

STUART IMMONEN
Artist

WADE VON GRAWBADGER
Inker

JUSTIN PONSOR
Colorist

CHRIS ELIOPOULOS
Letterer

IMMONEN, VON GRAWBADGER, PONSOR
Cover Artists

HEATHER ANTOS
Assistant Editor

JORDAN D. WHITE
Editor

C.B. CEBULSKI
Executive Editor

AXEL ALONSO
Editor In Chief

JOE QUESADA
Chief Creative Officer

DAN BUCKLEY
Publisher

For Lucasfilm:
Creative Director **MICHAEL SIGLAIN**
Senior Editor **FRANK PARISI**
Lucasfilm Story Group **RAYNE ROBERTS, PABLO HIDALGO, LELAND CHEE**

ABDO
Spotlight

ABDOPUBLISHING.COM

Reinforced library bound edition published in 2017 by Spotlight,
a division of ABDO, PO Box 398166, Minneapolis, Minnesota 55439.
Spotlight produces high-quality reinforced library bound editions for
schools and libraries. Published by agreement with Marvel Characters, Inc.

Printed in the United States of America, North Mankato, Minnesota.
092016
012017

THIS BOOK CONTAINS
RECYCLED MATERIALS

marvelkids.com

STAR WARS © & TM 2016 LUCASFILM LTD.

PUBLISHER'S CATALOGING IN PUBLICATION DATA

Names: Aaron, Jason, author. | Bianchi, Simone ; Ponsor, Justin ; Immonen, Stuart ;
    Von Grawbadger, Wade, illustrators.
Title: Showdown on the Smuggler's Moon / writer: Jason Aaron ; art: Simone
    Bianchi ; Justin Ponsor ; Stuart Immomen ; Wade Von Grawbadger.
Description: Reinforced library bound edition. | Minneapolis, Minnesota : Spotlight,
    2017. | Series: Star Wars : Showdown on the Smuggler's Moon
Summary: After reading Ben Kenobi's journal, Luke Skywalker is imprisoned during
    his search for a Jedi Temple, while Han and Leia flee from some Imperial troops
    with help from an unexpected foe, and Chewbacca and C-3PO are attacked by
    a mysterious bounty hunter.
Identifiers: LCCN 2016941802 | ISBN 9781614795544 (volume 1) | ISBN
    9781614795551 (volume 2) | ISBN 9781614795568 (volume 3) | ISBN
    9781614795575 (volume 4) | ISBN 9781614795582 (volume 5) | ISBN
    9781614795599 (volume 6)
Subjects: LCSH: Star Wars fiction--Comic books, strips, etc.--Juvenile fiction. |
    Graphic novels--Juvenile fiction.
Classification: DDC 741.5--dc23
LC record available at https://lccn.loc.gov/2016941802

Spotlight

A Division of ABDO
abdopublishing.com

WARS™

SHOWDOWN ON THE SMUGGLER'S MOON

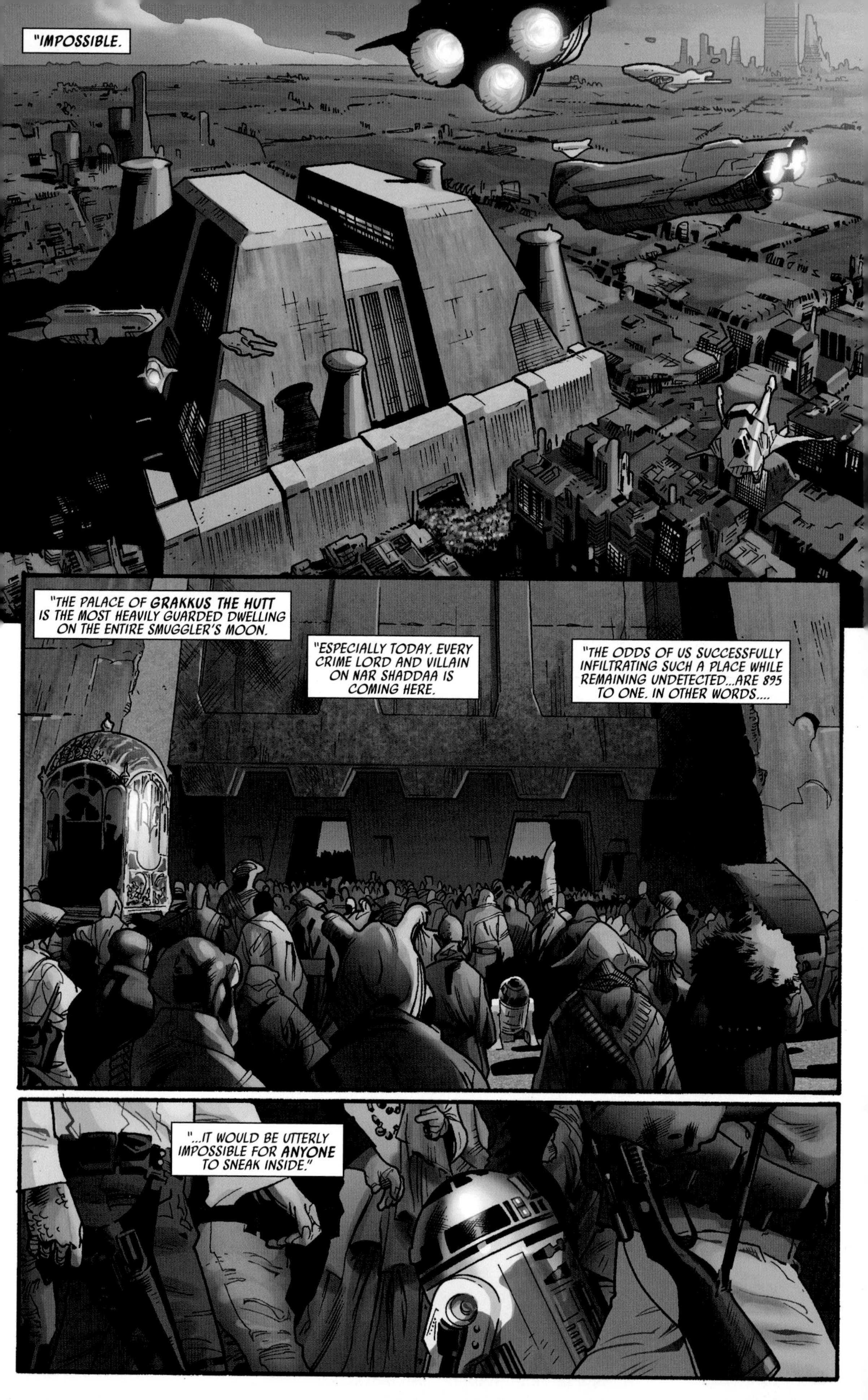
"IMPOSSIBLE.
"THE PALACE OF GRAKKUS THE HUTT IS THE MOST HEAVILY GUARDED DWELLING ON THE ENTIRE SMUGGLER'S MOON.
"ESPECIALLY TODAY. EVERY CRIME LORD AND VILLAIN ON NAR SHADDAA IS COMING HERE.
"THE ODDS OF US SUCCESSFULLY INFILTRATING SUCH A PLACE WHILE REMAINING UNDETECTED...ARE 895 TO ONE. IN OTHER WORDS....
"...IT WOULD BE UTTERLY IMPOSSIBLE FOR ANYONE TO SNEAK INSIDE."

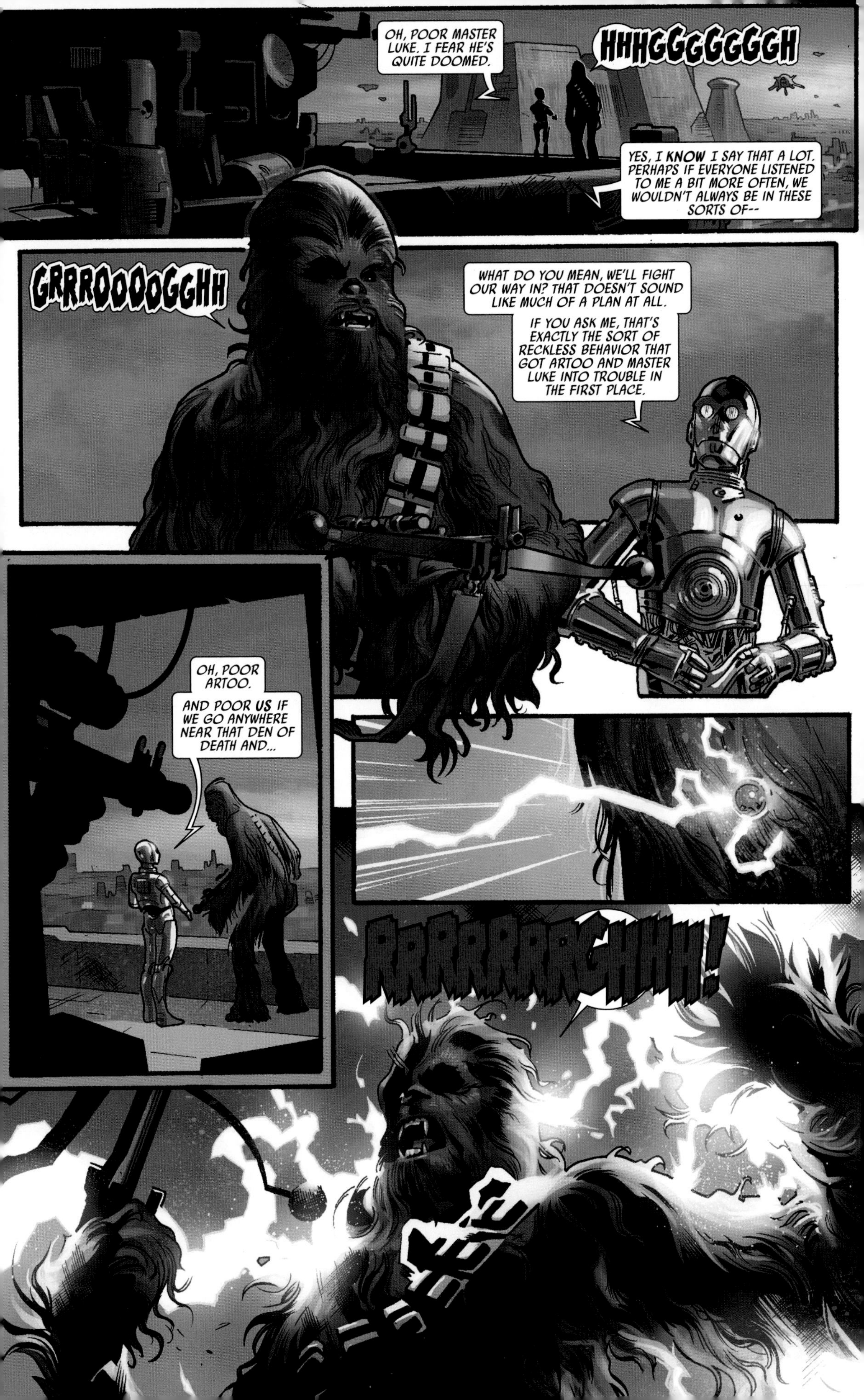
OH, POOR MASTER LUKE. I FEAR HE'S QUITE DOOMED.
HHHGGGGGGGH
YES, I KNOW I SAY THAT A LOT. PERHAPS IF EVERYONE LISTENED TO ME A BIT MORE OFTEN, WE WOULDN'T ALWAYS BE IN THESE SORTS OF--
GRRROOOOOGGHH
WHAT DO YOU MEAN, WE'LL FIGHT OUR WAY IN? THAT DOESN'T SOUND LIKE MUCH OF A PLAN AT ALL.
IF YOU ASK ME, THAT'S EXACTLY THE SORT OF RECKLESS BEHAVIOR THAT GOT ARTOO AND MASTER LUKE INTO TROUBLE IN THE FIRST PLACE.
OH, POOR ARTOO.
AND POOR US IF WE GO ANYWHERE NEAR THAT DEN OF DEATH AND...
RRRRRRRGHHH!

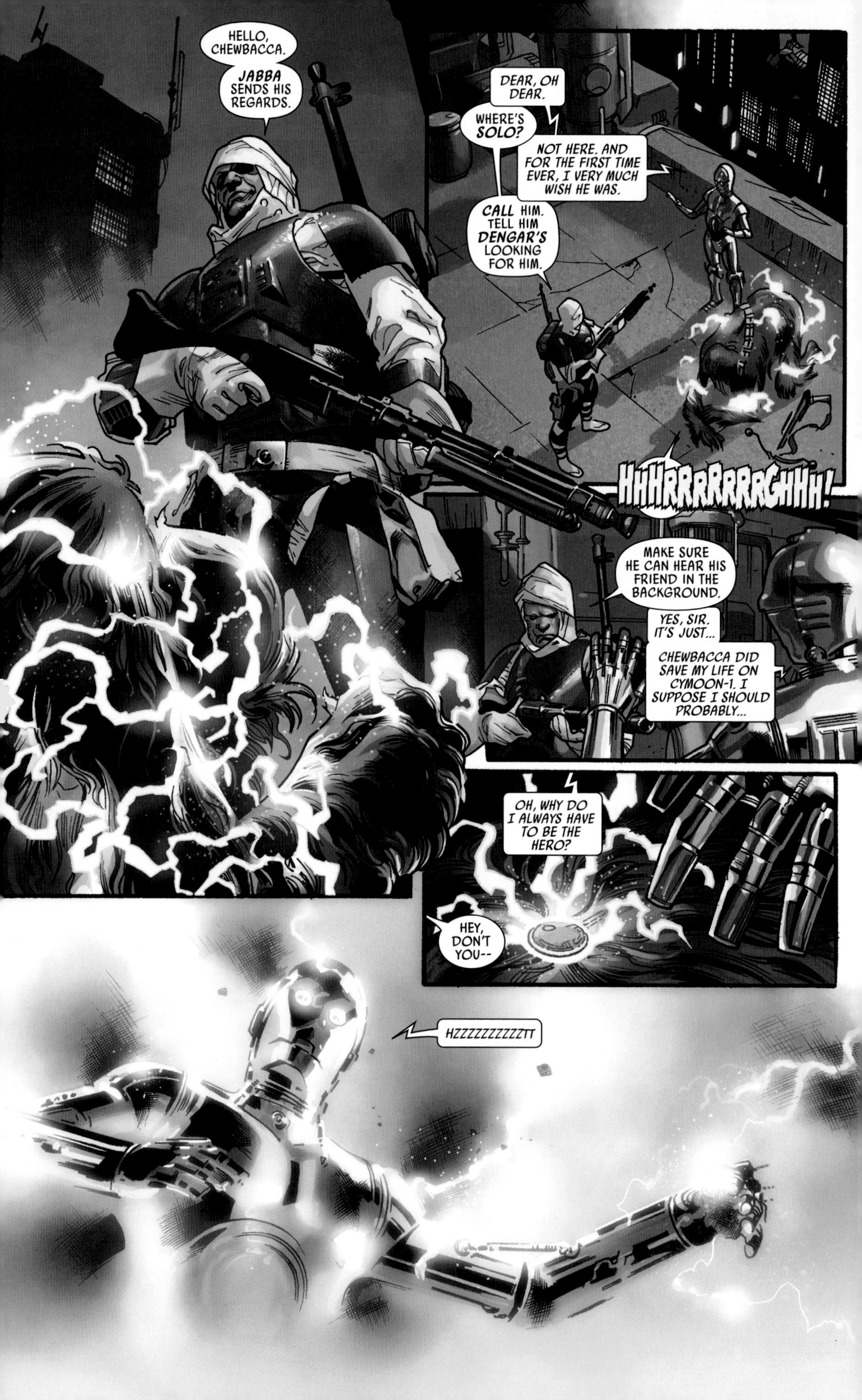

HELLO, CHEWBACCA.
JABBA SENDS HIS REGARDS.
DEAR, OH DEAR.
WHERE'S SOLO?
NOT HERE. AND FOR THE FIRST TIME EVER, I VERY MUCH WISH HE WAS.
CALL HIM. TELL HIM DENGAR'S LOOKING FOR HIM.
HHHRRRRRRRGHHH!
MAKE SURE HE CAN HEAR HIS FRIEND IN THE BACKGROUND.
YES, SIR. IT'S JUST...
CHEWBACCA DID SAVE MY LIFE ON CYMOON-1. I SUPPOSE I SHOULD PROBABLY...
OH, WHY DO I ALWAYS HAVE TO BE THE HERO?
HEY, DON'T YOU--
HZZZZZZZZZZTT

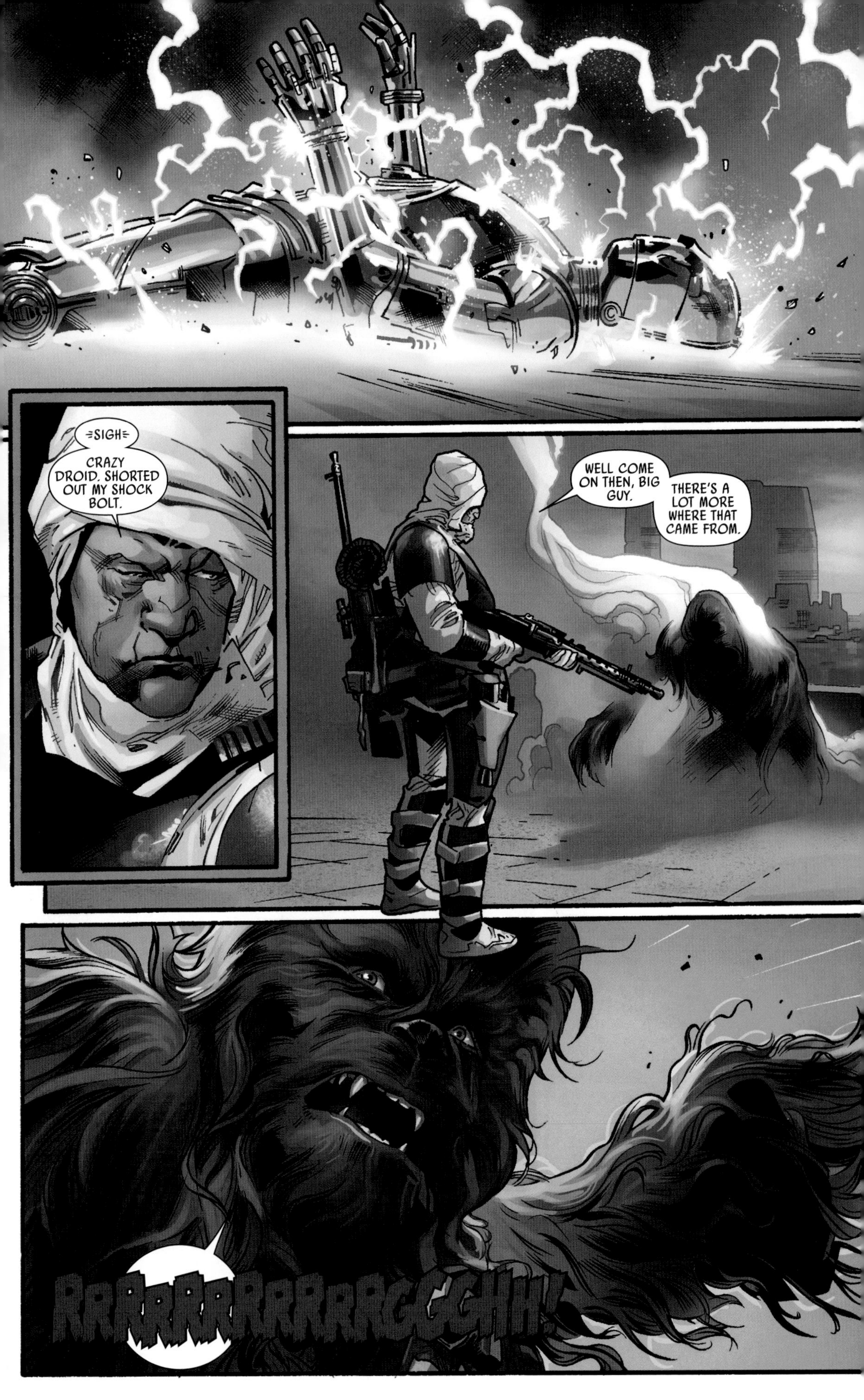

=SIGH=
CRAZY DROID. SHORTED OUT MY SHOCK BOLT.
WELL COME ON THEN, BIG GUY.
THERE'S A LOT MORE WHERE THAT CAME FROM.
RRRRRRRRRRRRRGGGHH!

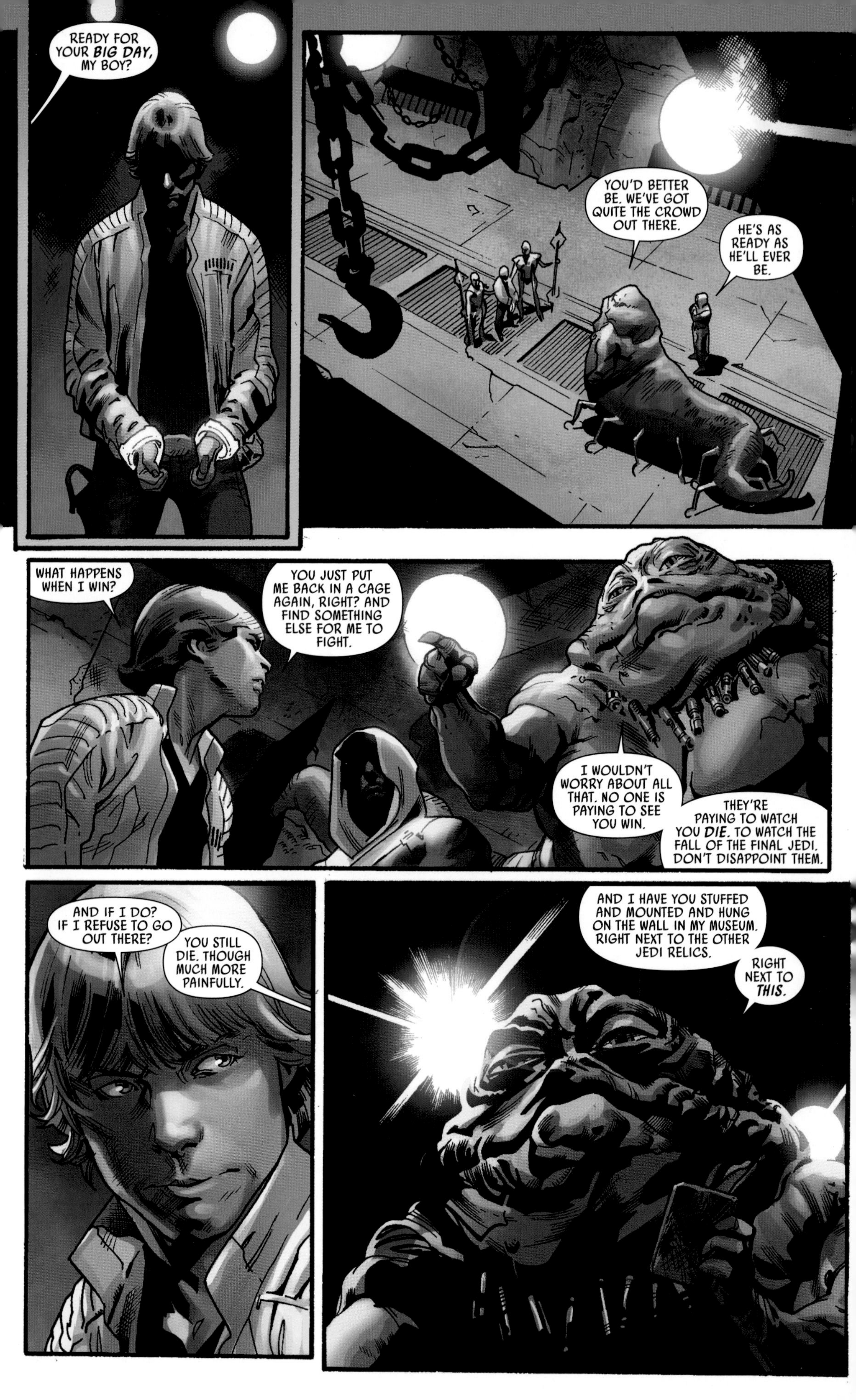
READY FOR YOUR BIG DAY, MY BOY?
YOU'D BETTER BE. WE'VE GOT QUITE THE CROWD OUT THERE.
HE'S AS READY AS HE'LL EVER BE.
WHAT HAPPENS WHEN I WIN?
YOU JUST PUT ME BACK IN A CAGE AGAIN, RIGHT? AND FIND SOMETHING ELSE FOR ME TO FIGHT.
I WOULDN'T WORRY ABOUT ALL THAT. NO ONE IS PAYING TO SEE YOU WIN.
THEY'RE PAYING TO WATCH YOU DIE. TO WATCH THE FALL OF THE FINAL JEDI. DON'T DISAPPOINT THEM.
AND IF I DO? IF I REFUSE TO GO OUT THERE?
YOU STILL DIE. THOUGH MUCH MORE PAINFULLY.
AND I HAVE YOU STUFFED AND MOUNTED AND HUNG ON THE WALL IN MY MUSEUM. RIGHT NEXT TO THE OTHER JEDI RELICS.
RIGHT NEXT TO THIS.

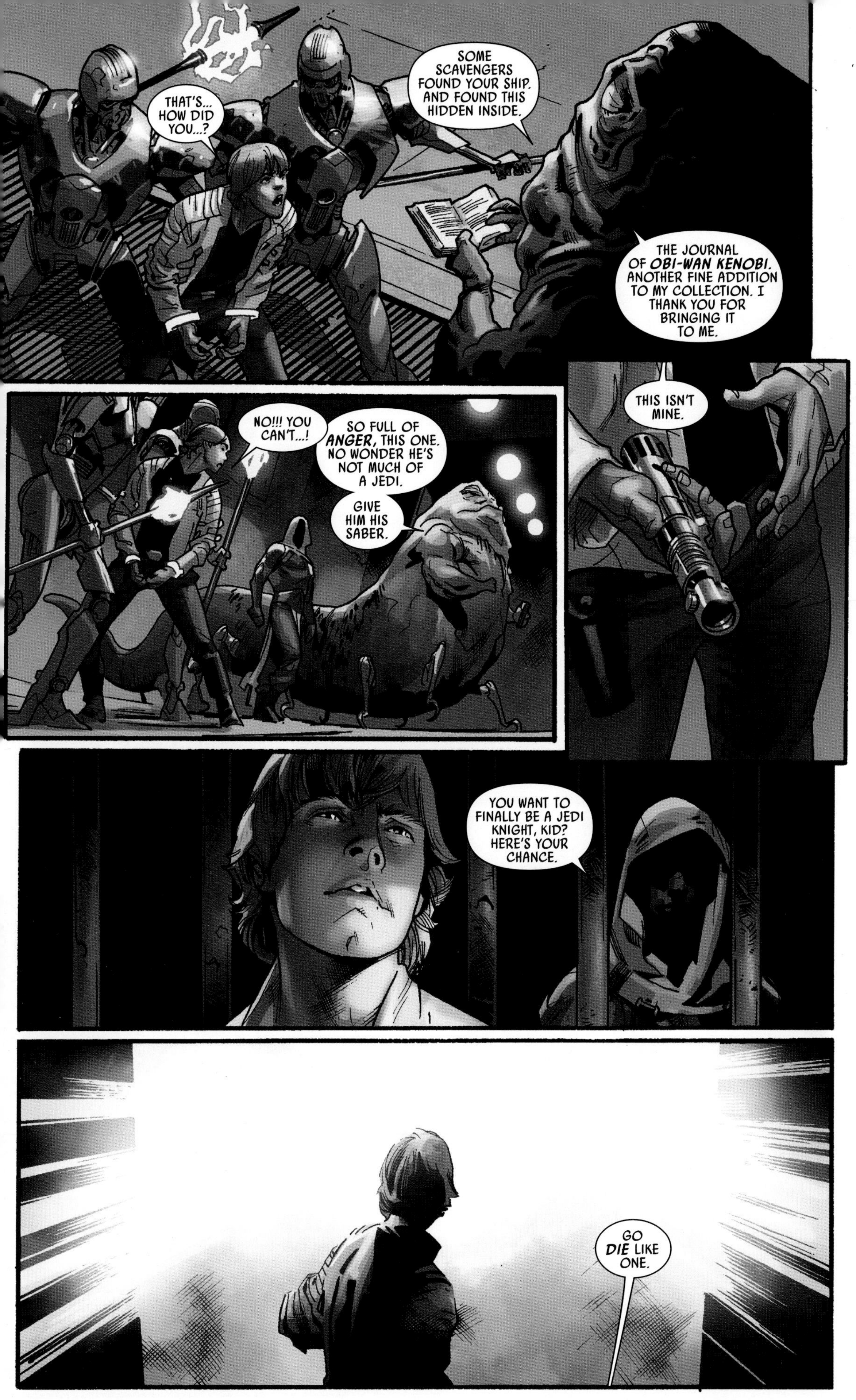
THAT'S... HOW DID YOU...?
SOME SCAVENGERS FOUND YOUR SHIP. AND FOUND THIS HIDDEN INSIDE.
THE JOURNAL OF OBI-WAN KENOBI. ANOTHER FINE ADDITION TO MY COLLECTION. I THANK YOU FOR BRINGING IT TO ME.
NO!!! YOU CAN'T...!
SO FULL OF ANGER, THIS ONE. NO WONDER HE'S NOT MUCH OF A JEDI.
GIVE HIM HIS SABER.
THIS ISN'T MINE.
YOU WANT TO FINALLY BE A JEDI KNIGHT, KID? HERE'S YOUR CHANCE.
GO DIE LIKE ONE.

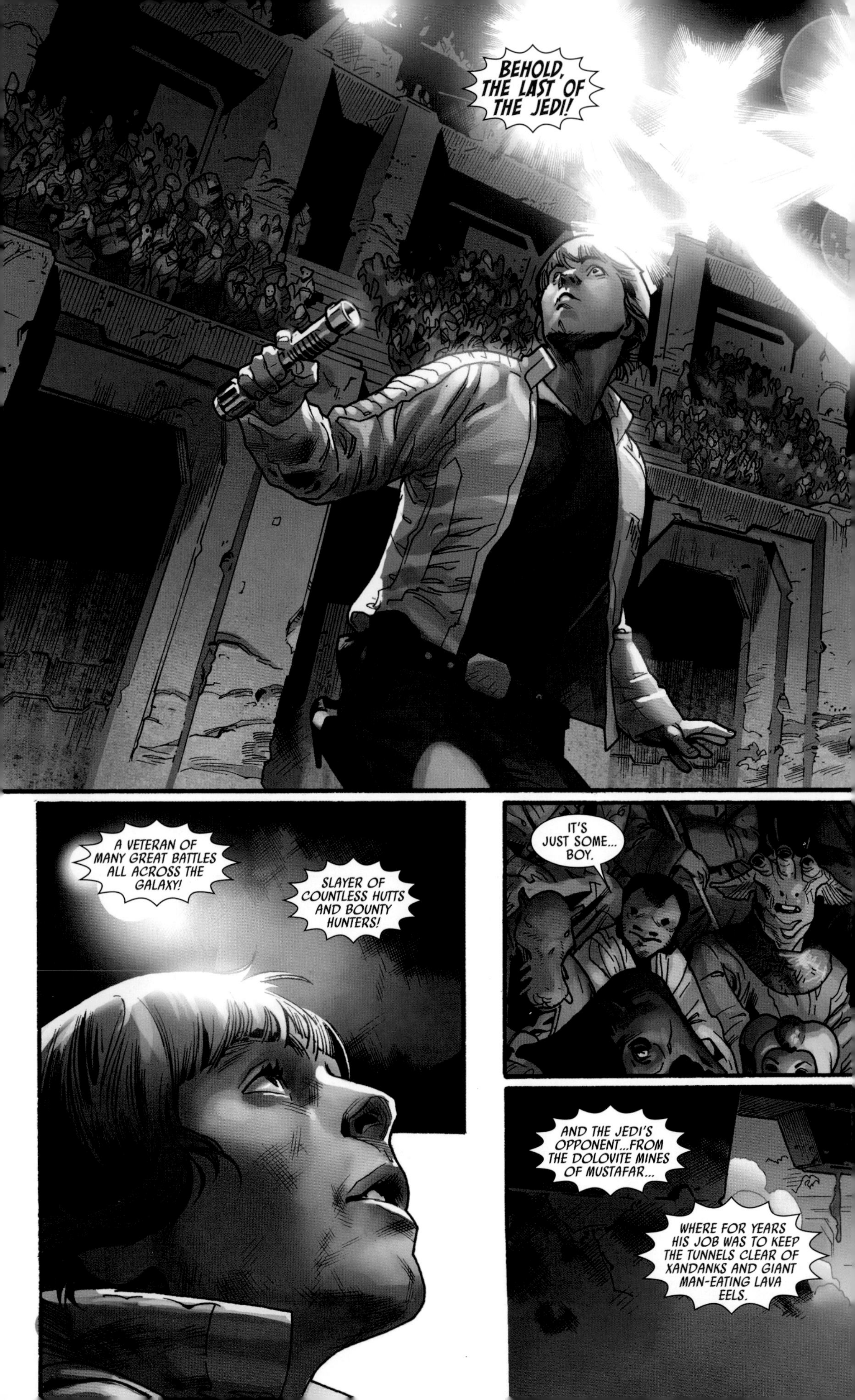
BEHOLD, THE LAST OF THE JEDI!
A VETERAN OF MANY GREAT BATTLES ALL ACROSS THE GALAXY!
SLAYER OF COUNTLESS HUTTS AND BOUNTY HUNTERS!
IT'S JUST SOME... BOY.
AND THE JEDI'S OPPONENT...FROM THE DOLOVITE MINES OF MUSTAFAR...
WHERE FOR YEARS HIS JOB WAS TO KEEP THE TUNNELS CLEAR OF XANDANKS AND GIANT MAN-EATING LAVA EELS.

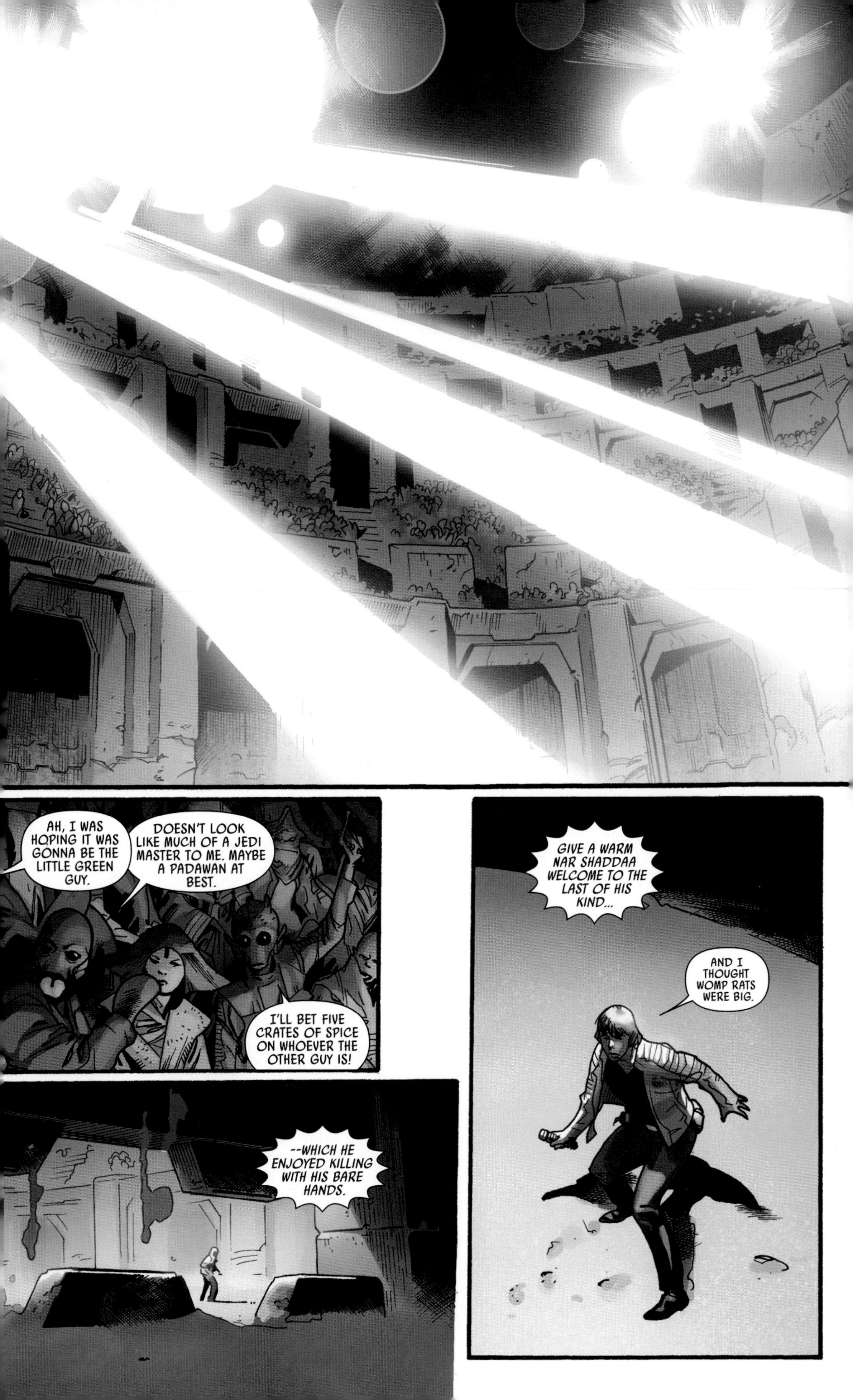
AH, I WAS HOPING IT WAS GONNA BE THE LITTLE GREEN GUY.
DOESN'T LOOK LIKE MUCH OF A JEDI MASTER TO ME. MAYBE A PADAWAN AT BEST.
I'LL BET FIVE CRATES OF SPICE ON WHOEVER THE OTHER GUY IS!
--WHICH HE ENJOYED KILLING WITH HIS BARE HANDS.
GIVE A WARM NAR SHADDAA WELCOME TO THE LAST OF HIS KIND...
AND I THOUGHT WOMP RATS WERE BIG.

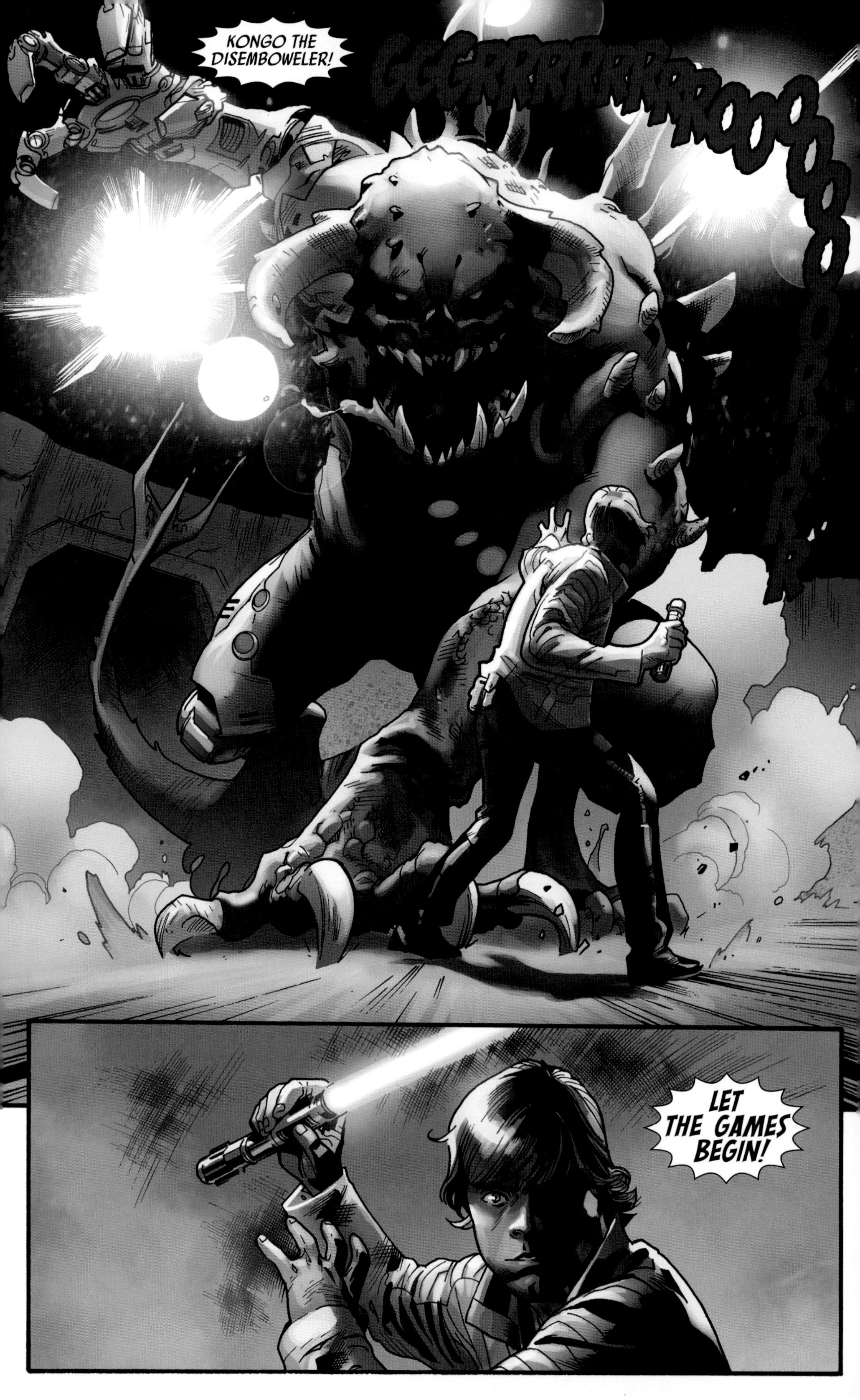
KONGO THE DISEMBOWELER!
GGGRRRRRRRRROOOOOOOOOOORRRRR
LET THE GAMES BEGIN!

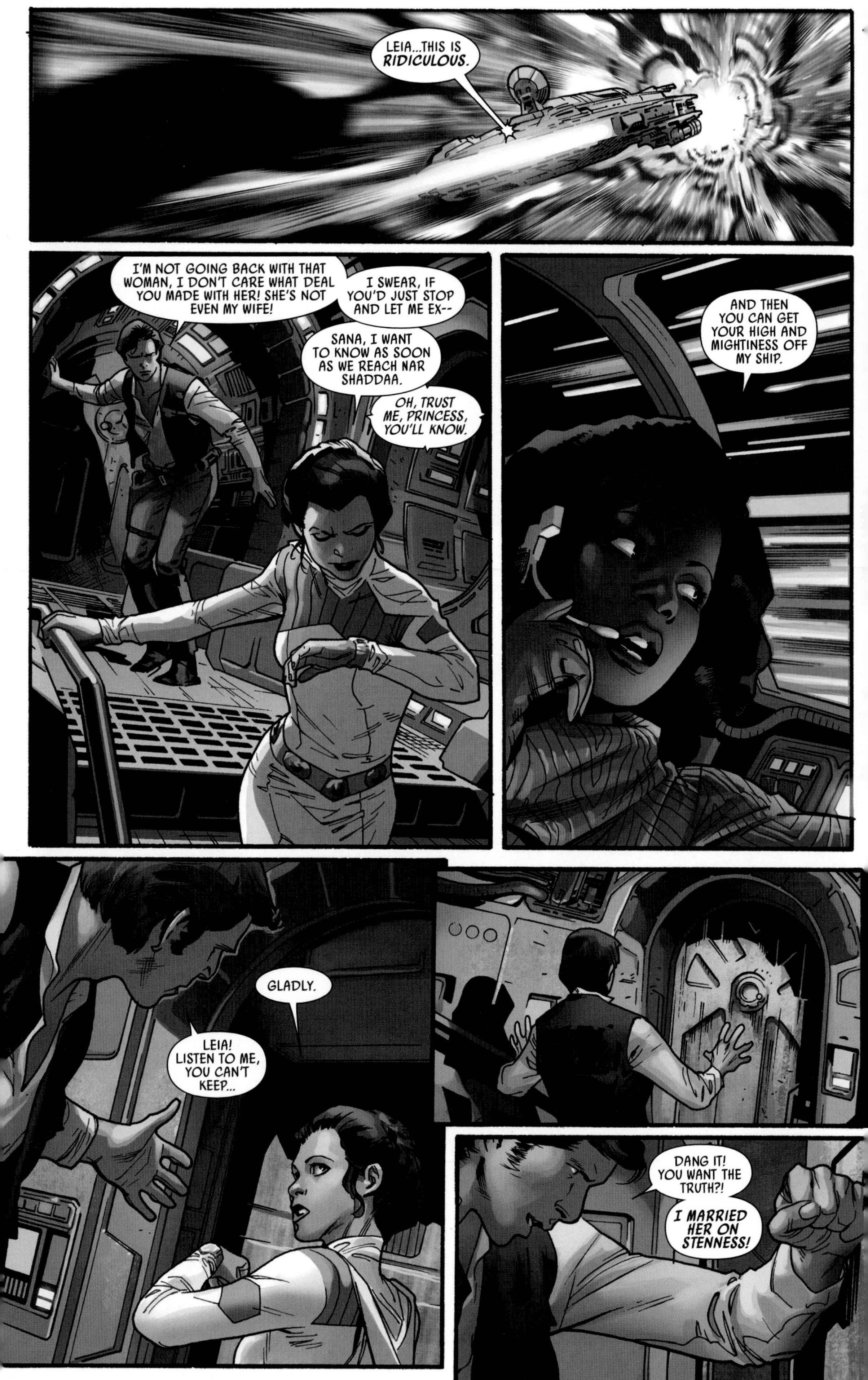
LEIA...THIS IS RIDICULOUS.
I'M NOT GOING BACK WITH THAT WOMAN, I DON'T CARE WHAT DEAL YOU MADE WITH HER! SHE'S NOT EVEN MY WIFE!
I SWEAR, IF YOU'D JUST STOP AND LET ME EX--
SANA, I WANT TO KNOW AS SOON AS WE REACH NAR SHADDAA.
OH, TRUST ME, PRINCESS, YOU'LL KNOW.
AND THEN YOU CAN GET YOUR HIGH AND MIGHTINESS OFF MY SHIP.
GLADLY.
LEIA! LISTEN TO ME, YOU CAN'T KEEP...
DANG IT! YOU WANT THE TRUTH?!
I MARRIED HER ON STENNESS!

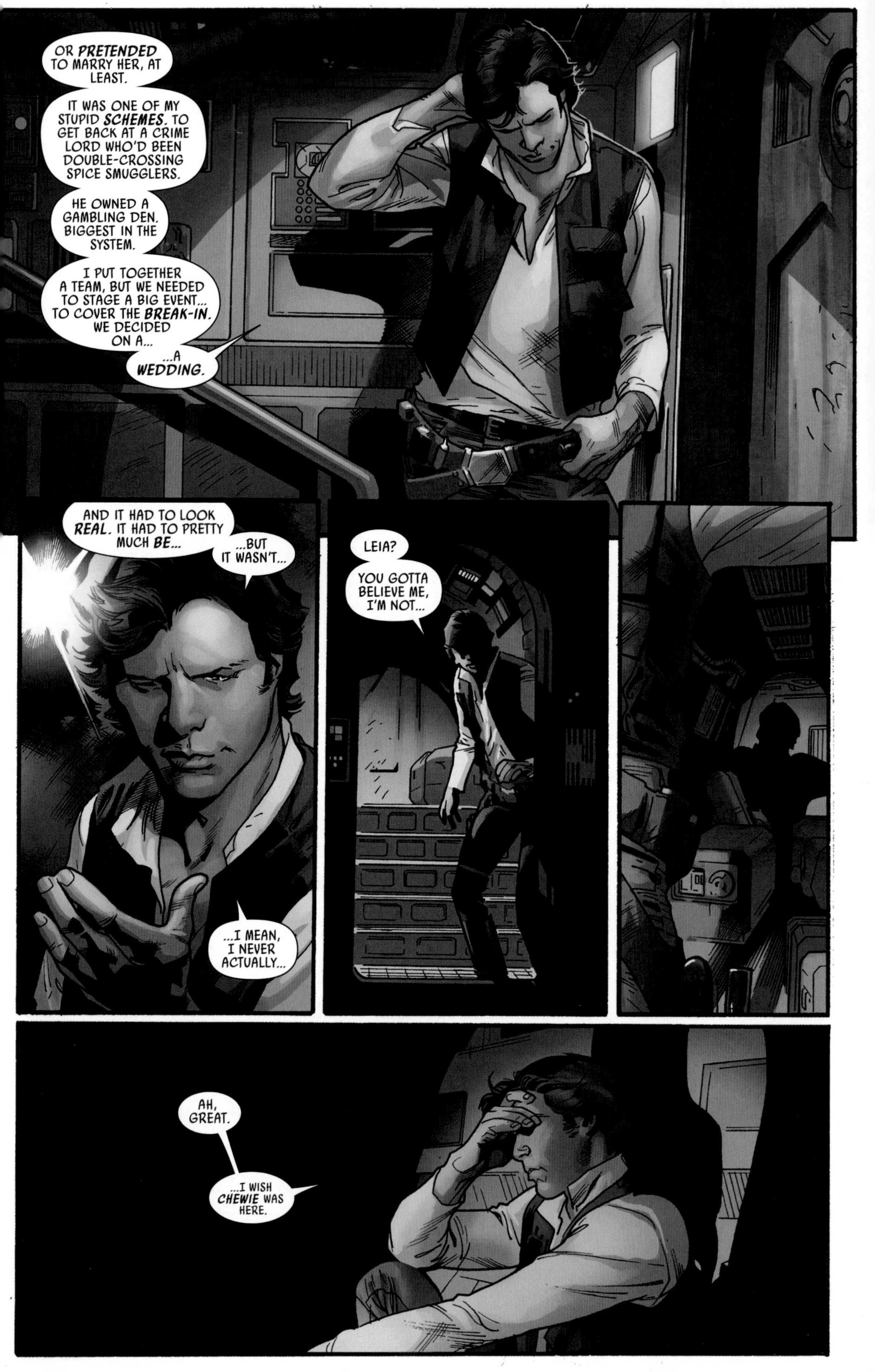
OR PRETENDED TO MARRY HER, AT LEAST.
IT WAS ONE OF MY STUPID SCHEMES. TO GET BACK AT A CRIME LORD WHO'D BEEN DOUBLE-CROSSING SPICE SMUGGLERS.
HE OWNED A GAMBLING DEN. BIGGEST IN THE SYSTEM.
I PUT TOGETHER A TEAM, BUT WE NEEDED TO STAGE A BIG EVENT... TO COVER THE BREAK-IN. WE DECIDED ON A...
...A WEDDING.
AND IT HAD TO LOOK REAL. IT HAD TO PRETTY MUCH BE...
...BUT IT WASN'T...
...I MEAN, I NEVER ACTUALLY...
LEIA?
YOU GOTTA BELIEVE ME, I'M NOT...
AH, GREAT.
...I WISH CHEWIE WAS HERE.

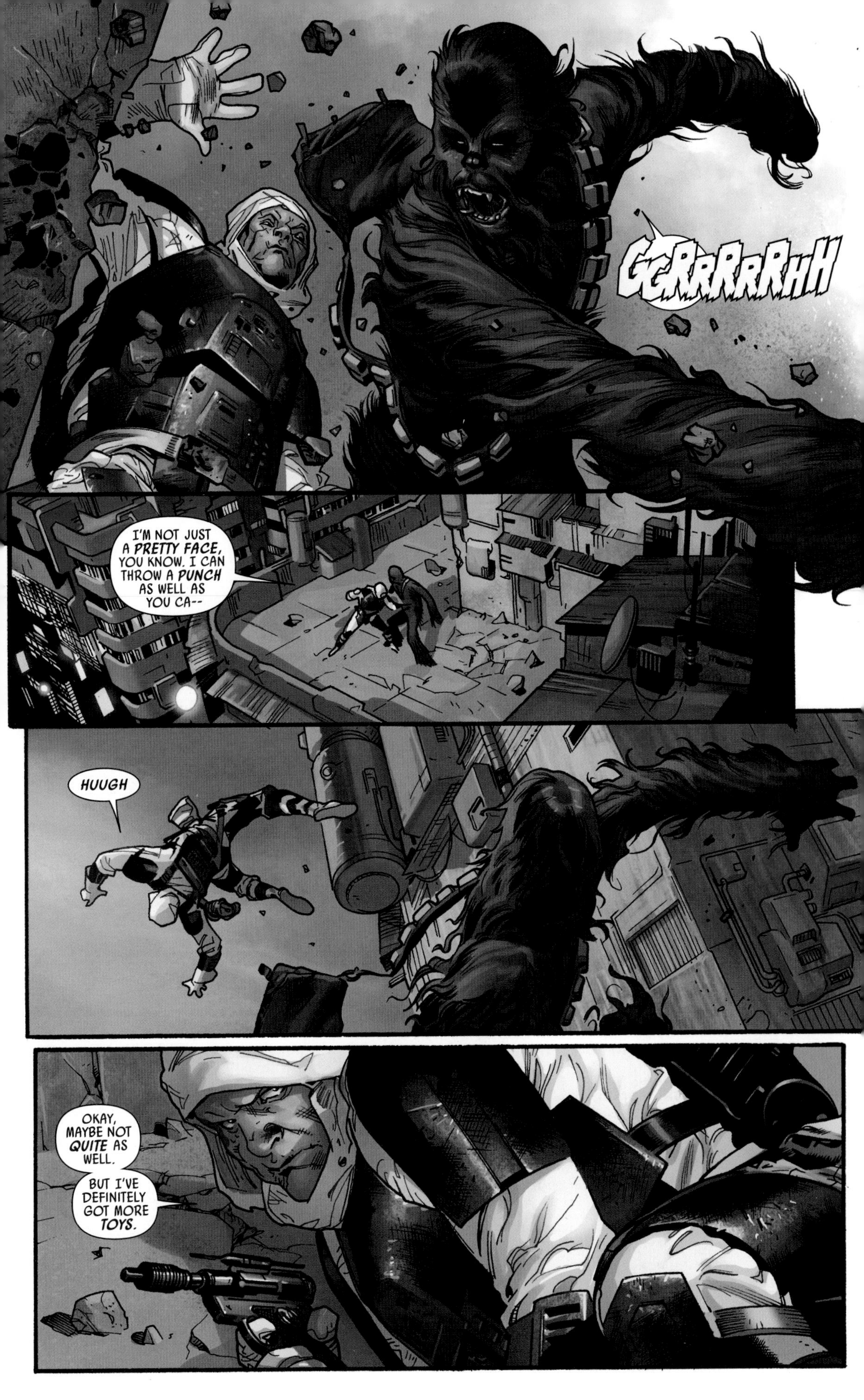
GGRRRRRRHH
I'M NOT JUST A PRETTY FACE, YOU KNOW. I CAN THROW A PUNCH AS WELL AS YOU CA--
HUUGH
OKAY, MAYBE NOT QUITE AS WELL.
BUT I'VE DEFINITELY GOT MORE TOYS.

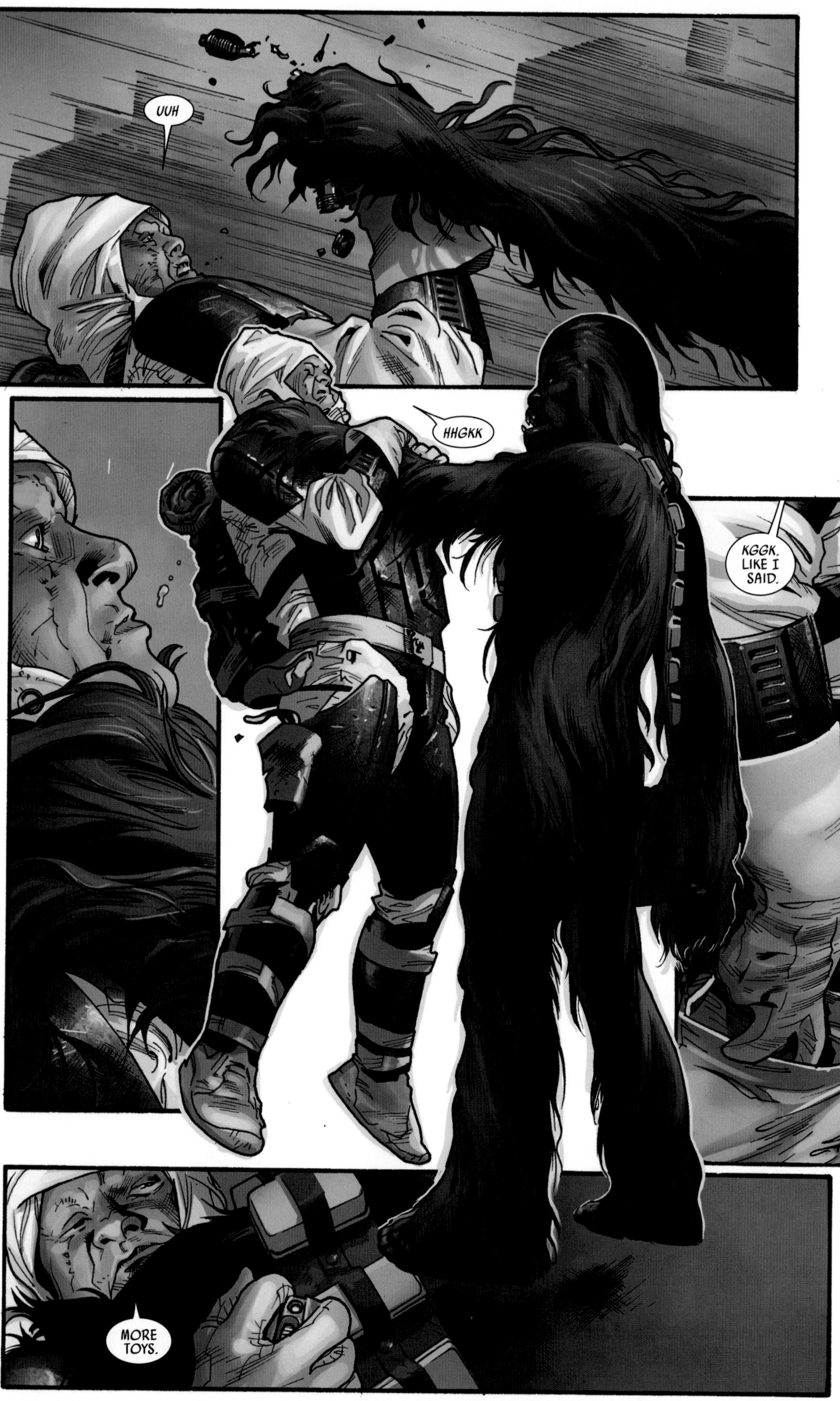
UUH
HHGKK
KGGK. LIKE I SAID.
MORE TOYS.

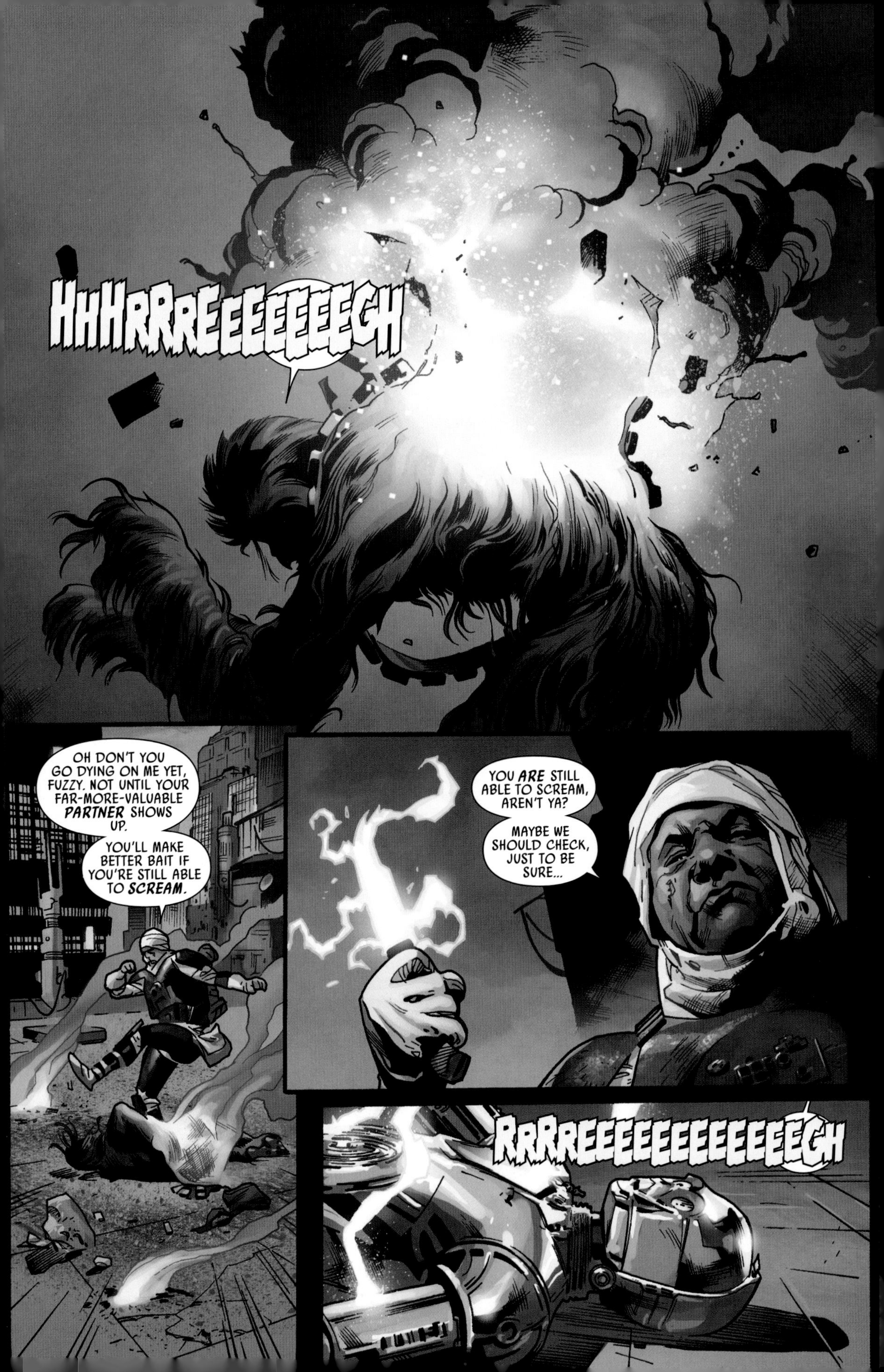
HHHRRREEEEEEEEGH
OH DON'T YOU GO DYING ON ME YET, FUZZY. NOT UNTIL YOUR FAR-MORE-VALUABLE PARTNER SHOWS UP.
YOU'LL MAKE BETTER BAIT IF YOU'RE STILL ABLE TO SCREAM.
YOU ARE STILL ABLE TO SCREAM, AREN'T YA?
MAYBE WE SHOULD CHECK, JUST TO BE SURE...
RRRREEEEEEEEEEEEEGH

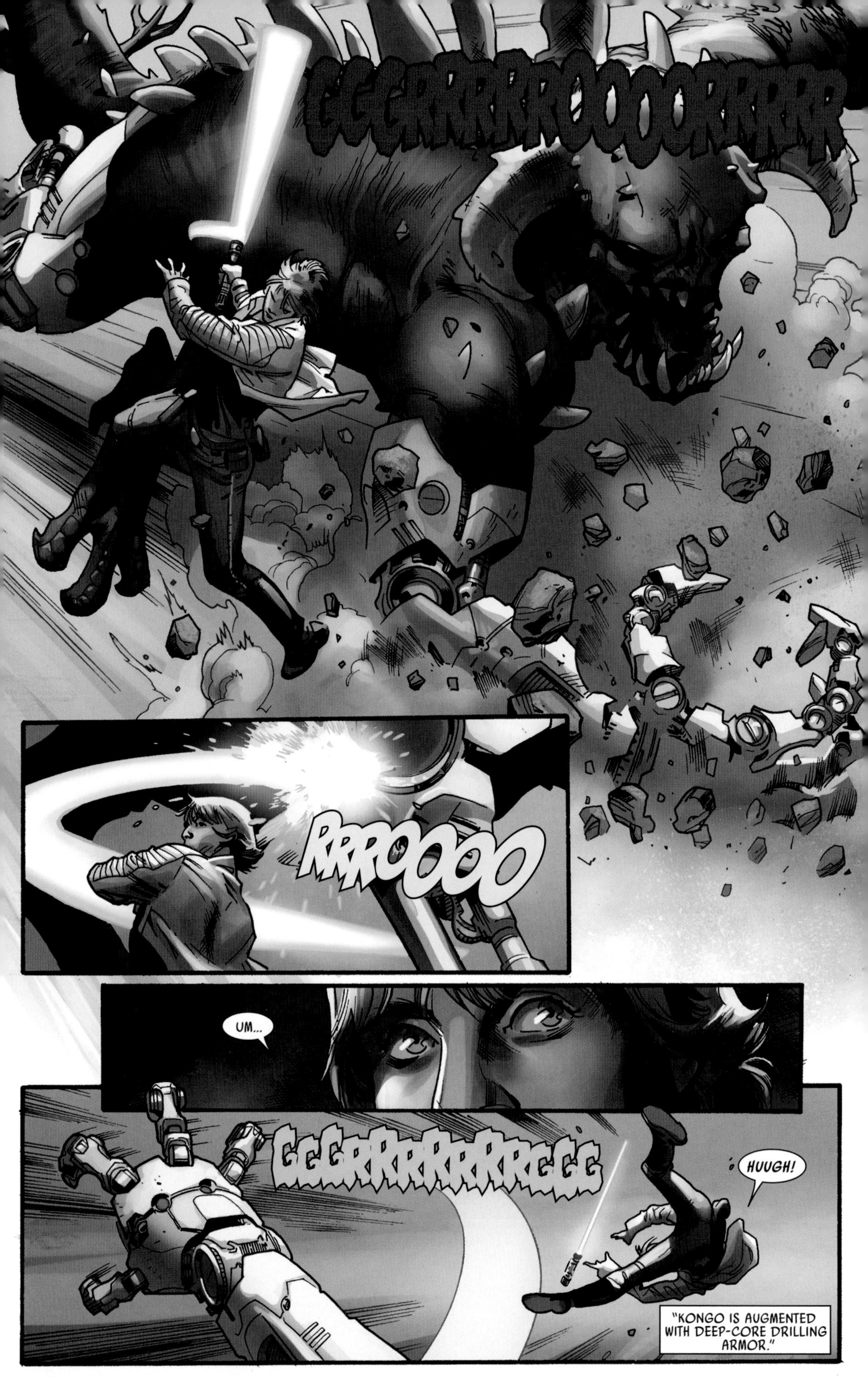
GGGRRRRRRROOOORRRRR
RRROOOOO
UM...
GGGRRRRRRRRRGGG
HUUGH!
"KONGO IS AUGMENTED WITH DEEP-CORE DRILLING ARMOR."

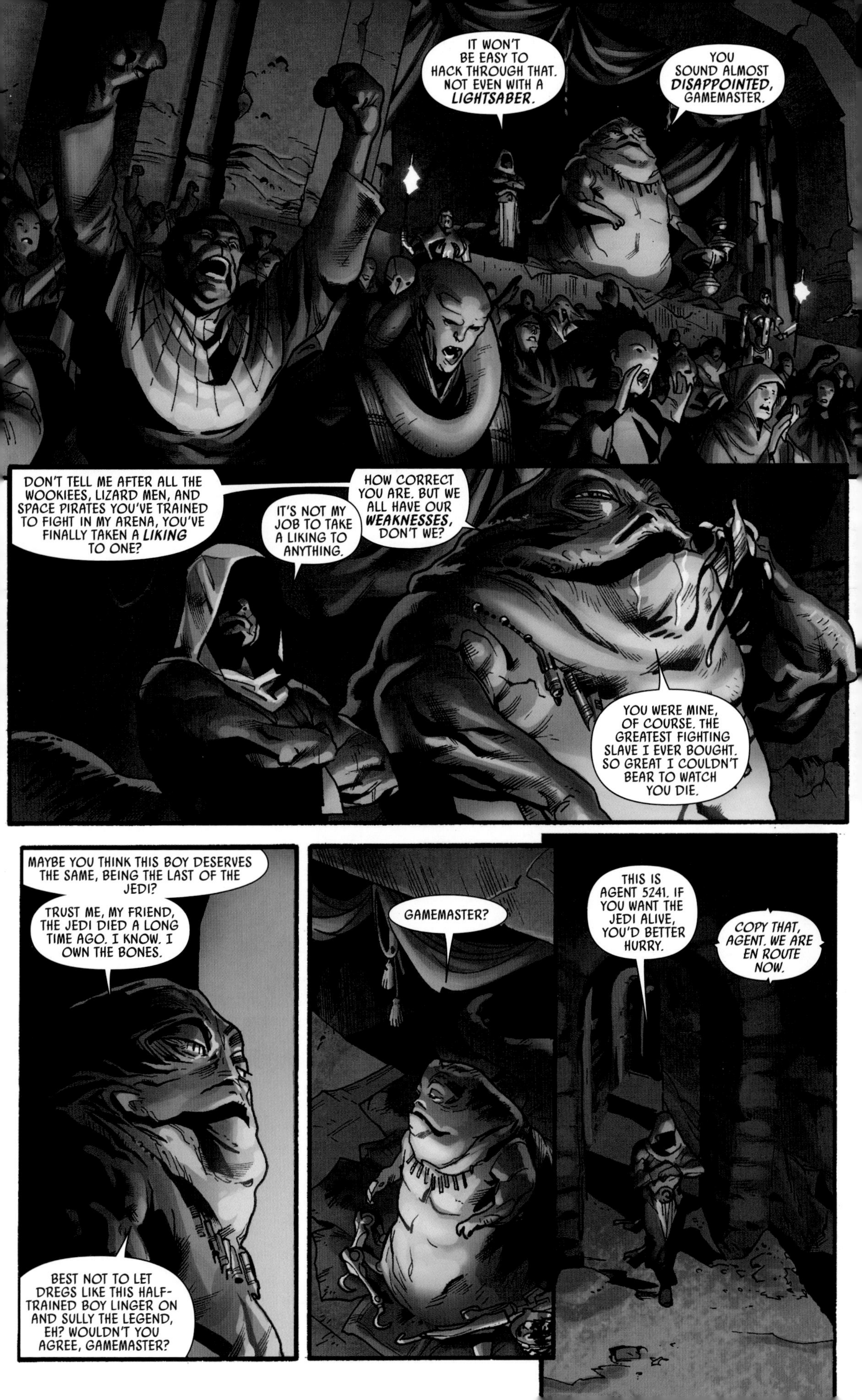
IT WON'T BE EASY TO HACK THROUGH THAT. NOT EVEN WITH A LIGHTSABER.
YOU SOUND ALMOST DISAPPOINTED, GAMEMASTER.
DON'T TELL ME AFTER ALL THE WOOKIEES, LIZARD MEN, AND SPACE PIRATES YOU'VE TRAINED TO FIGHT IN MY ARENA, YOU'VE FINALLY TAKEN A LIKING TO ONE?
IT'S NOT MY JOB TO TAKE A LIKING TO ANYTHING.
HOW CORRECT YOU ARE. BUT WE ALL HAVE OUR WEAKNESSES, DON'T WE?
YOU WERE MINE, OF COURSE. THE GREATEST FIGHTING SLAVE I EVER BOUGHT. SO GREAT I COULDN'T BEAR TO WATCH YOU DIE.
MAYBE YOU THINK THIS BOY DESERVES THE SAME, BEING THE LAST OF THE JEDI?
TRUST ME, MY FRIEND, THE JEDI DIED A LONG TIME AGO. I KNOW. I OWN THE BONES.
BEST NOT TO LET DREGS LIKE THIS HALF-TRAINED BOY LINGER ON AND SULLY THE LEGEND, EH? WOULDN'T YOU AGREE, GAMEMASTER?
GAMEMASTER?
THIS IS AGENT 5241. IF YOU WANT THE JEDI ALIVE, YOU'D BETTER HURRY.
COPY THAT, AGENT. WE ARE EN ROUTE NOW.

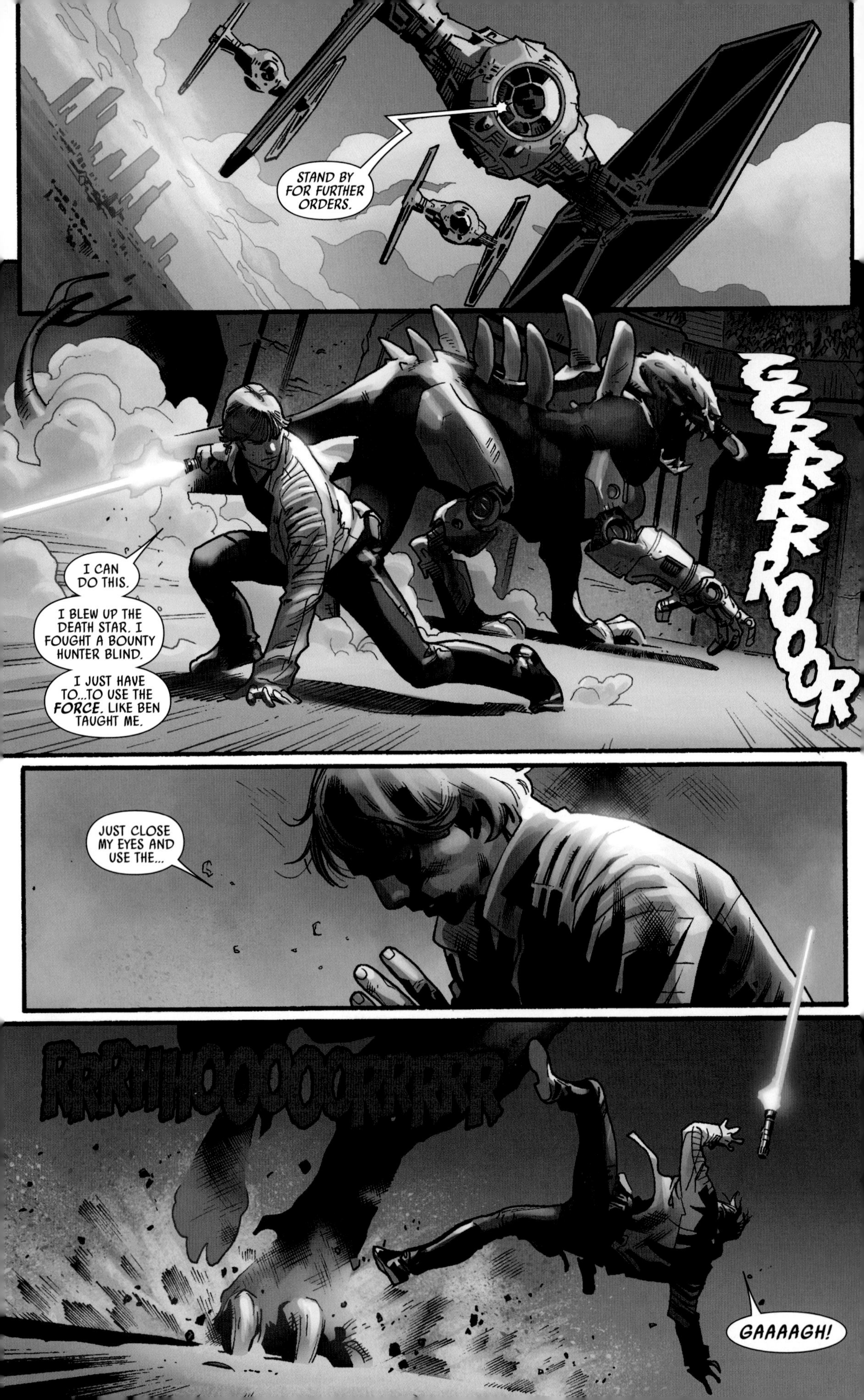
STAND BY FOR FURTHER ORDERS.
GGRRRROOOR
I CAN DO THIS.
I BLEW UP THE DEATH STAR. I FOUGHT A BOUNTY HUNTER BLIND.
I JUST HAVE TO...TO USE THE FORCE. LIKE BEN TAUGHT ME.
JUST CLOSE MY EYES AND USE THE...
RRRHHOOOOORRRRR
GAAAAGH!

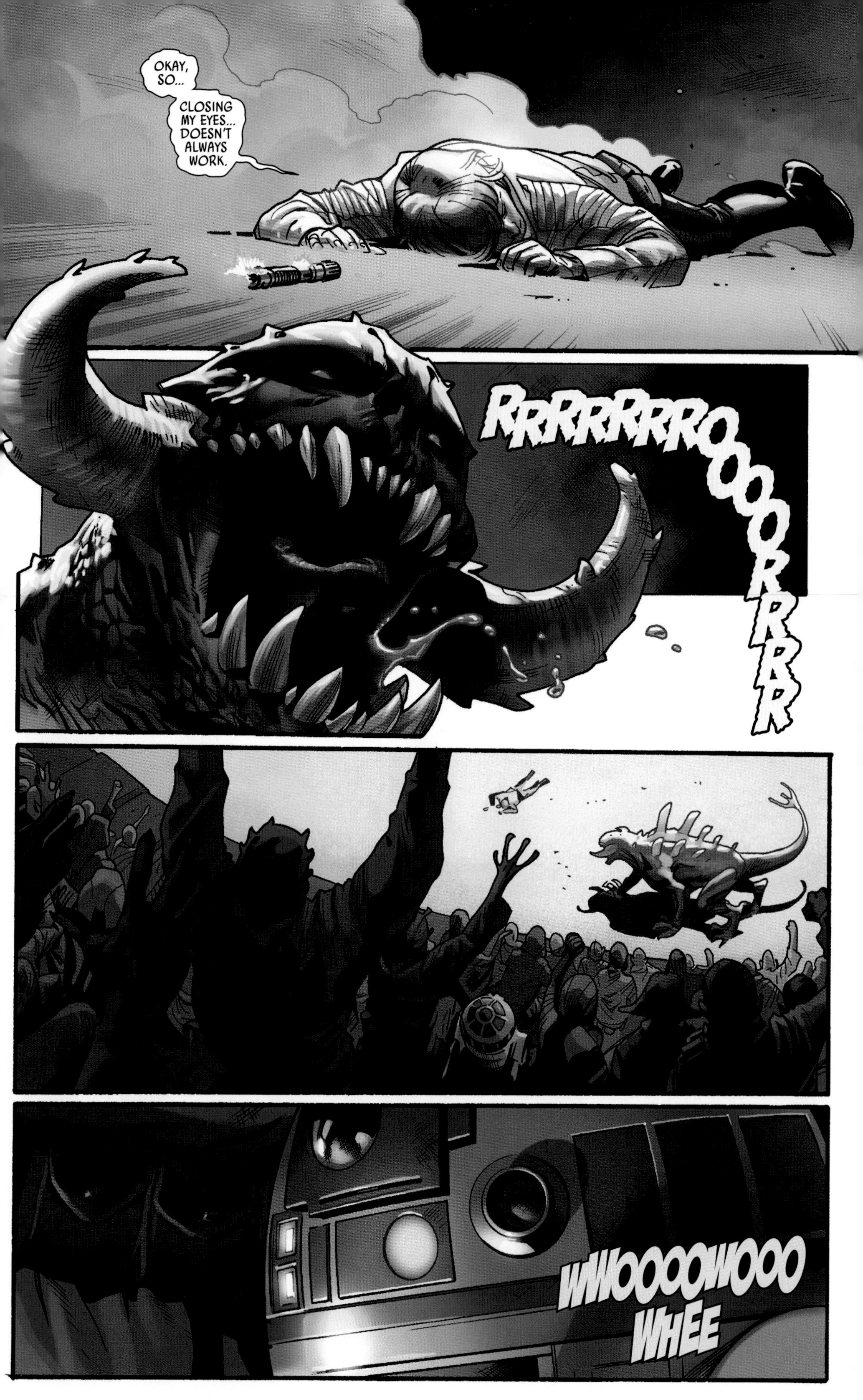
OKAY, SO...
CLOSING MY EYES... DOESN'T ALWAYS WORK.
RRRRRRROOOOORRRRR
WWOOOOWOOO WHEE

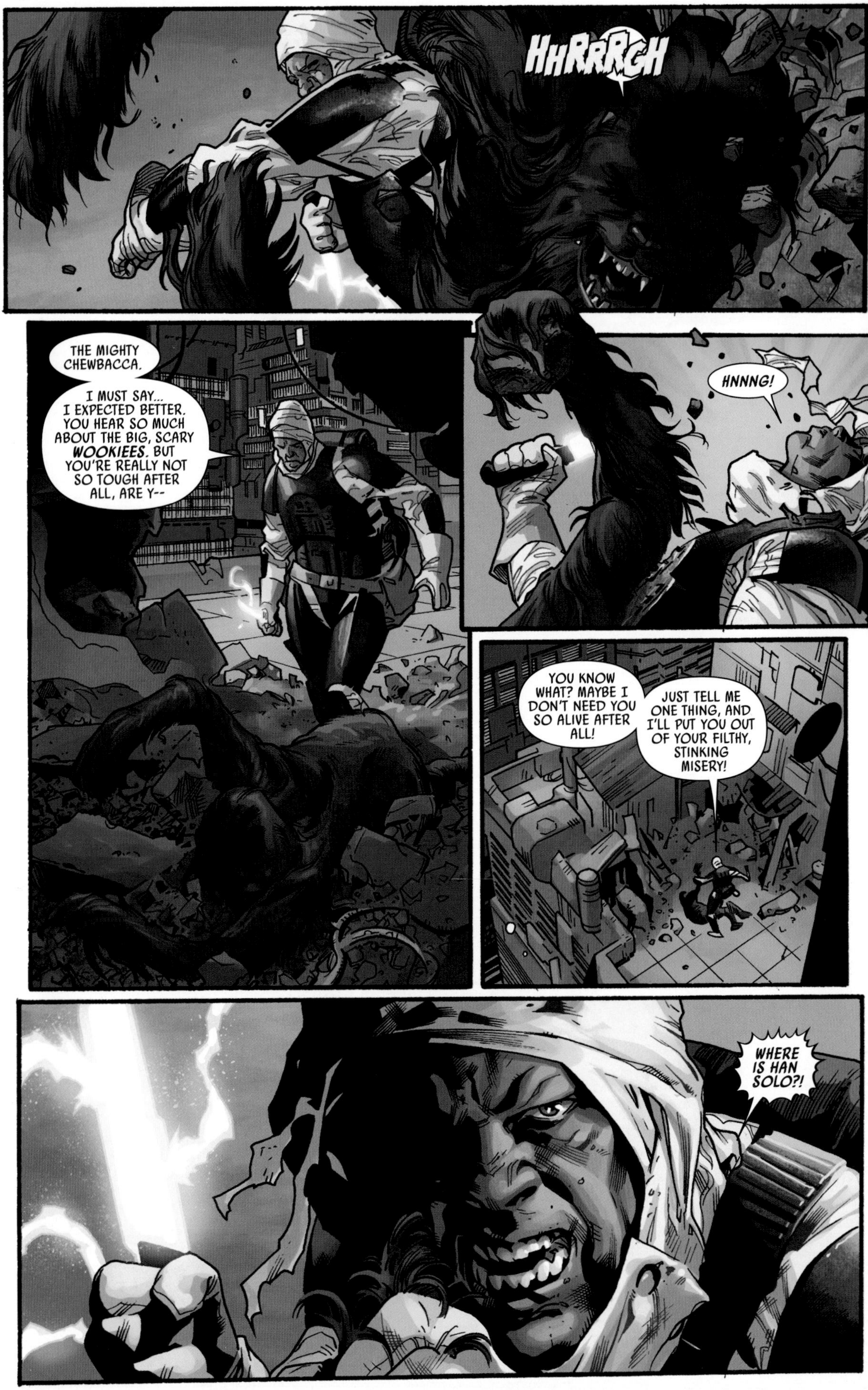
HHRRRGH
THE MIGHTY CHEWBACCA.
I MUST SAY... I EXPECTED BETTER. YOU HEAR SO MUCH ABOUT THE BIG, SCARY WOOKIEES. BUT YOU'RE REALLY NOT SO TOUGH AFTER ALL, ARE Y--
HNNNG!
YOU KNOW WHAT? MAYBE I DON'T NEED YOU SO ALIVE AFTER ALL!
JUST TELL ME ONE THING, AND I'LL PUT YOU OUT OF YOUR FILTHY, STINKING MISERY!
WHERE IS HAN SOLO?!

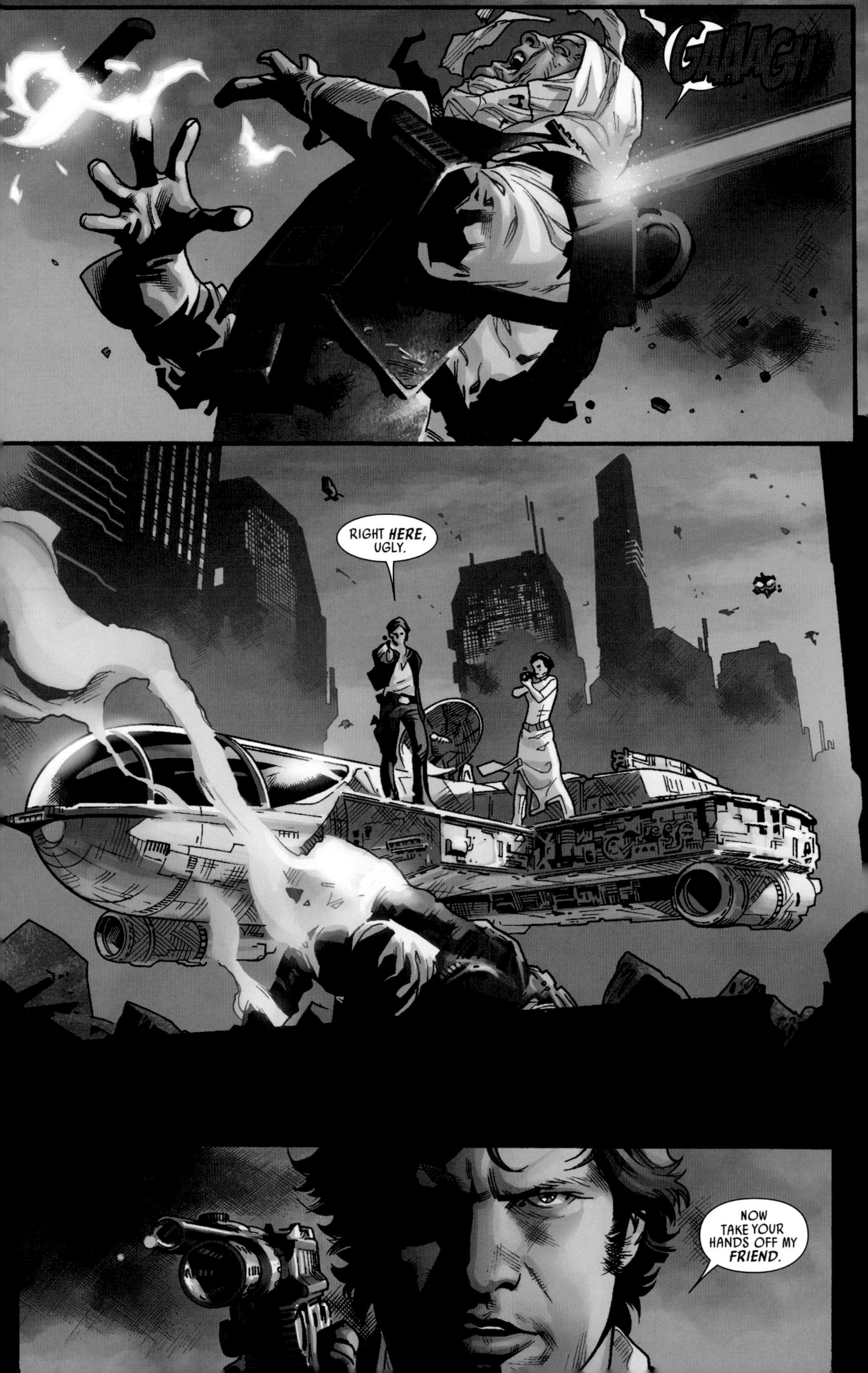
RIGHT *HERE*, UGLY.
NOW TAKE YOUR HANDS OFF MY *FRIEND*.

STAR WARS™

SHOWDOWN ON THE SMUGGLER'S MOON

COLLECT THEM ALL!

Set of 6 Hardcover Books ISBN: 978-1-61479-553-7

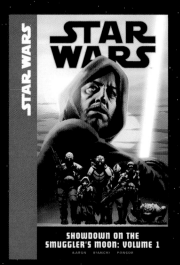

Hardcover Book ISBN
978-1-61479-554-4

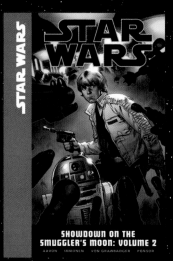

Hardcover Book ISBN
978-1-61479-555-1

Hardcover Book ISBN
978-1-61479-556-8

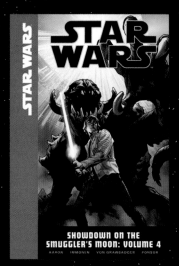

Hardcover Book ISBN
978-1-61479-557-5

Hardcover Book ISBN
978-1-61479-558-2

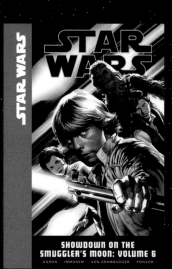

Hardcover Book ISBN
978-1-61479-559-9